To my kind-hearted, curious explorers, Fisher & Crosby.
—CP

To my wise, adventurous journey companion & sister, Erin.
—MD

BOOKS of GREAT CHARACTER

TOO MANY BUBBLES

A Story about Mindfulness

Words by

CHRISTINE PECK
& MAGS DEROMA

Pictures by

MAGS DEROMA

sourcebooks
jabberwocky

It all started with a thought.

A sort of grumpy one.

One little thought bubble.

It bubbled up one day, a rough day, and just hung there.

It followed Izzy around, hovering, all day, until it was time for bed.

And when Izzy woke up the next day, it was still there.

And maybe a little bigger.

And definitely not alone.

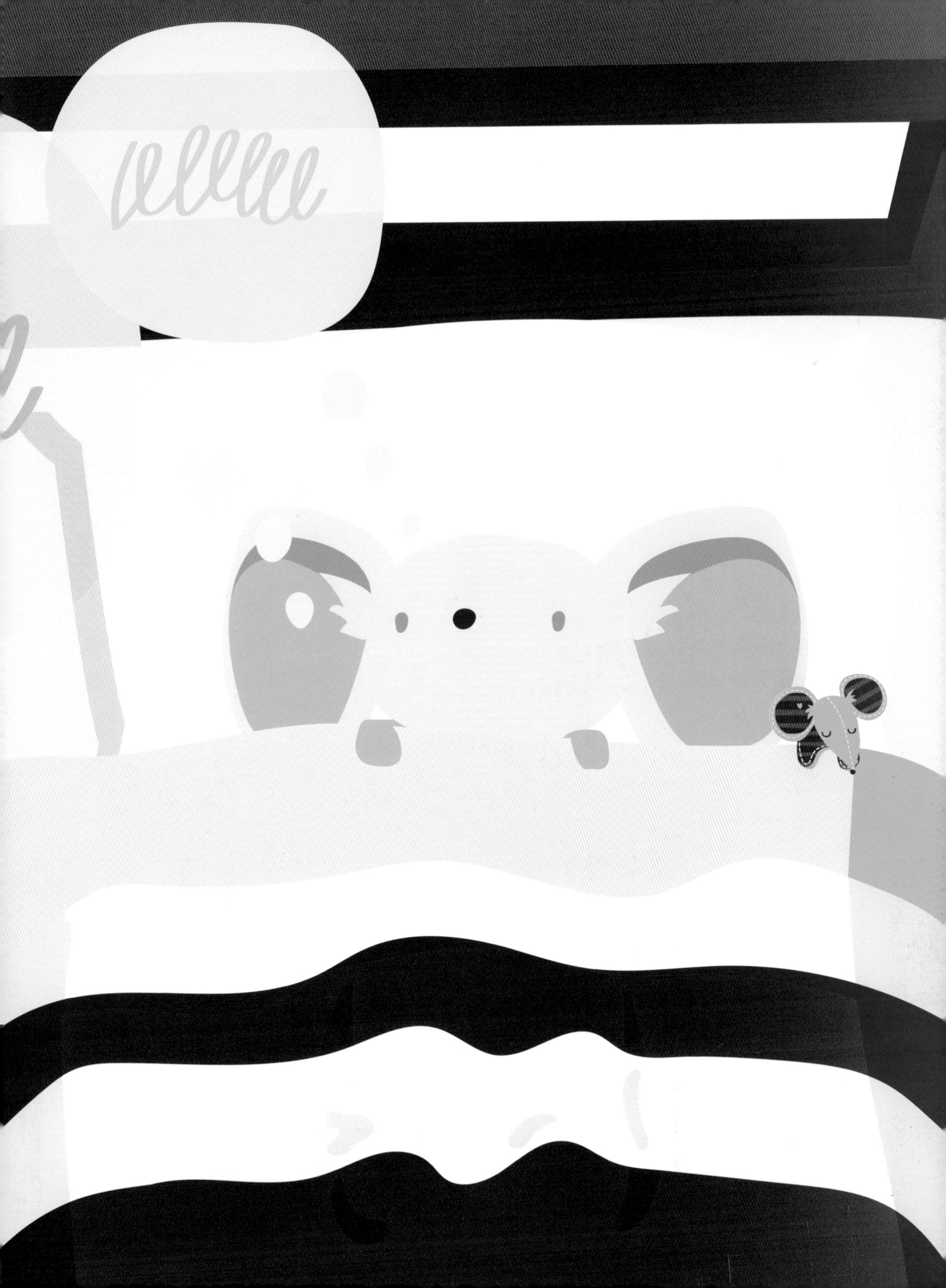

At first, it was simply peculiar.

But when another popped up, and another,
and another, they started to really
get in the way of things.

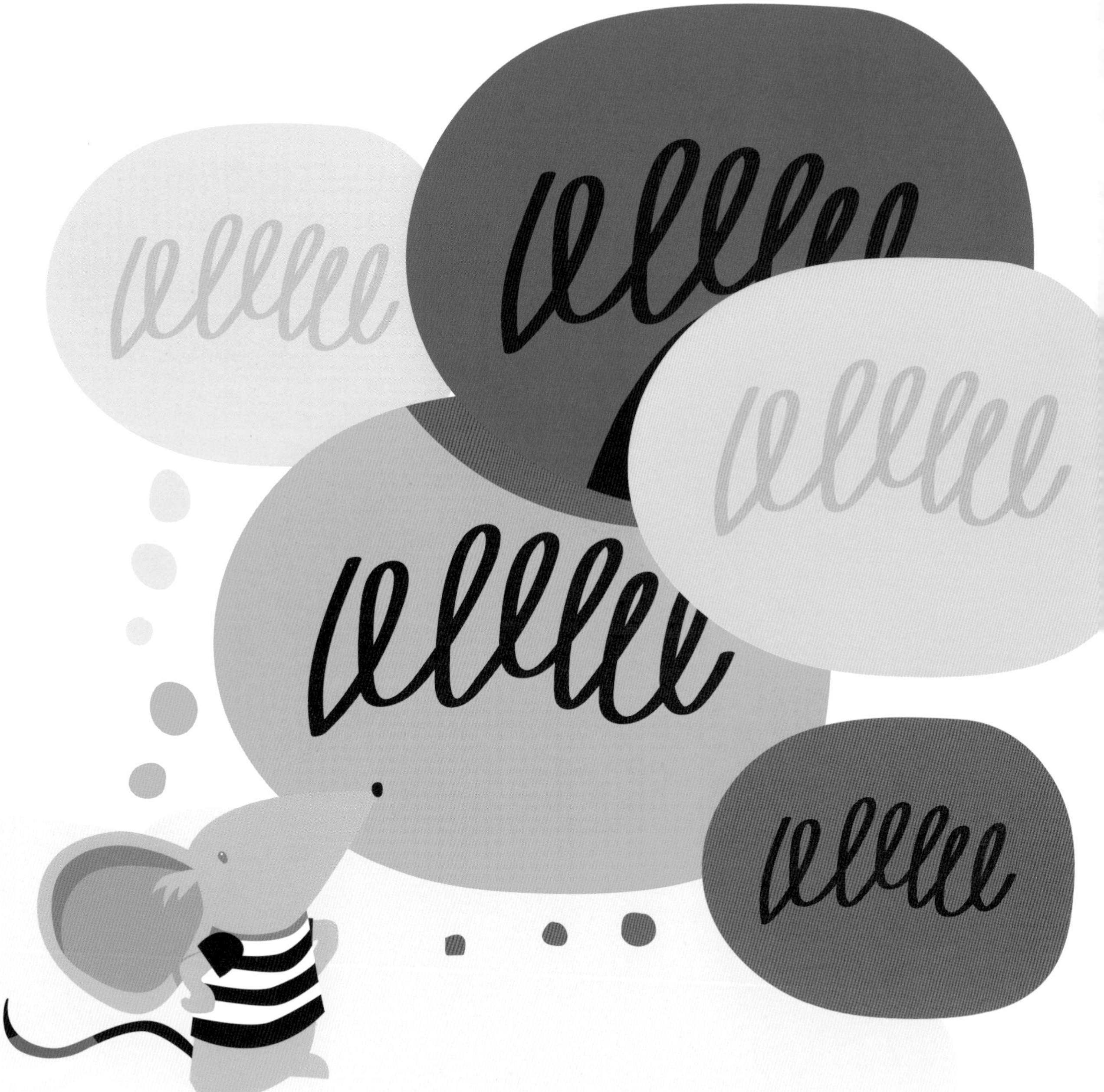

They cast a shadow on Izzy's day.

A super shadowy shadow.

More kept *pop-pop-popping* up,

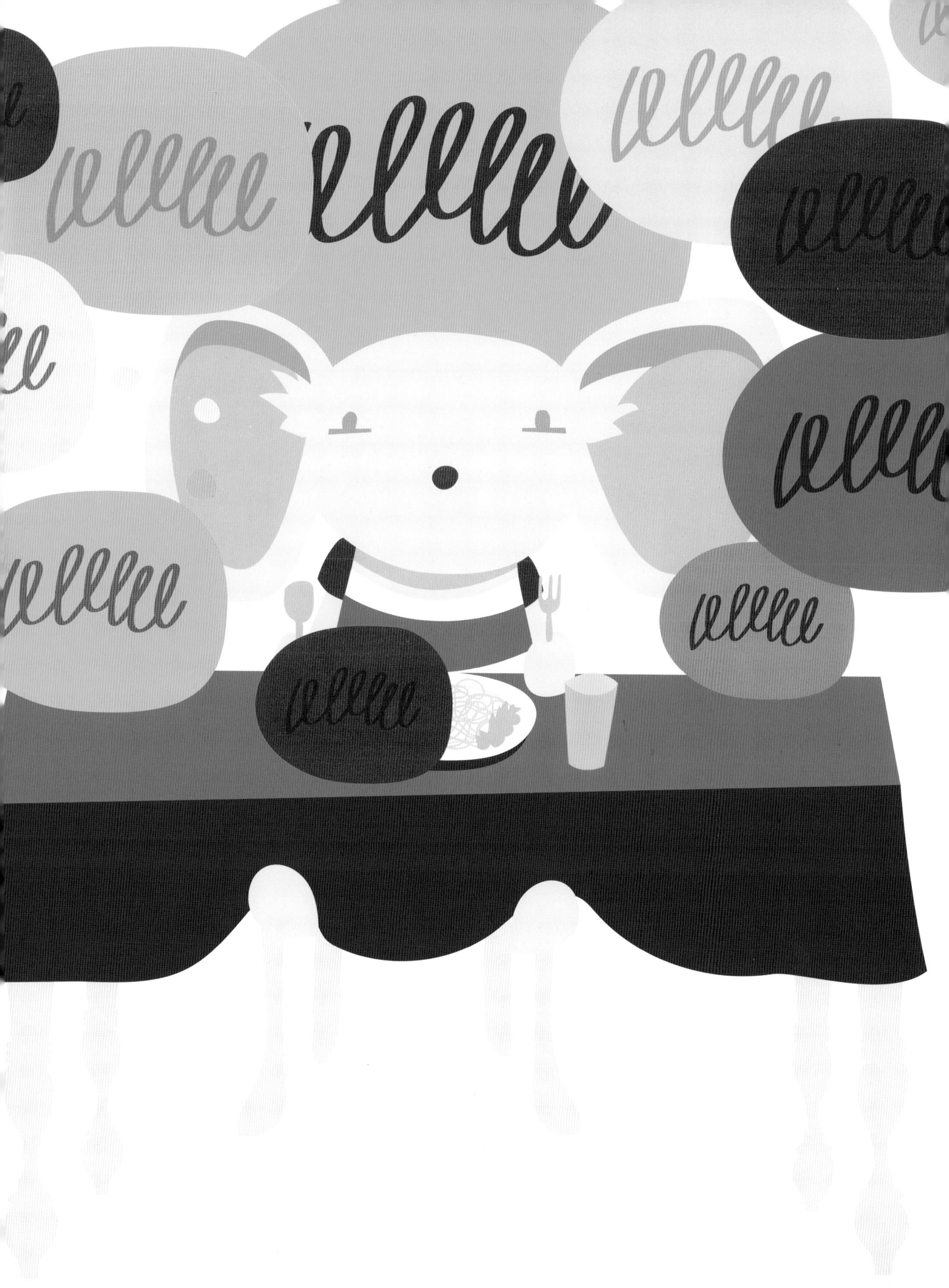

until...

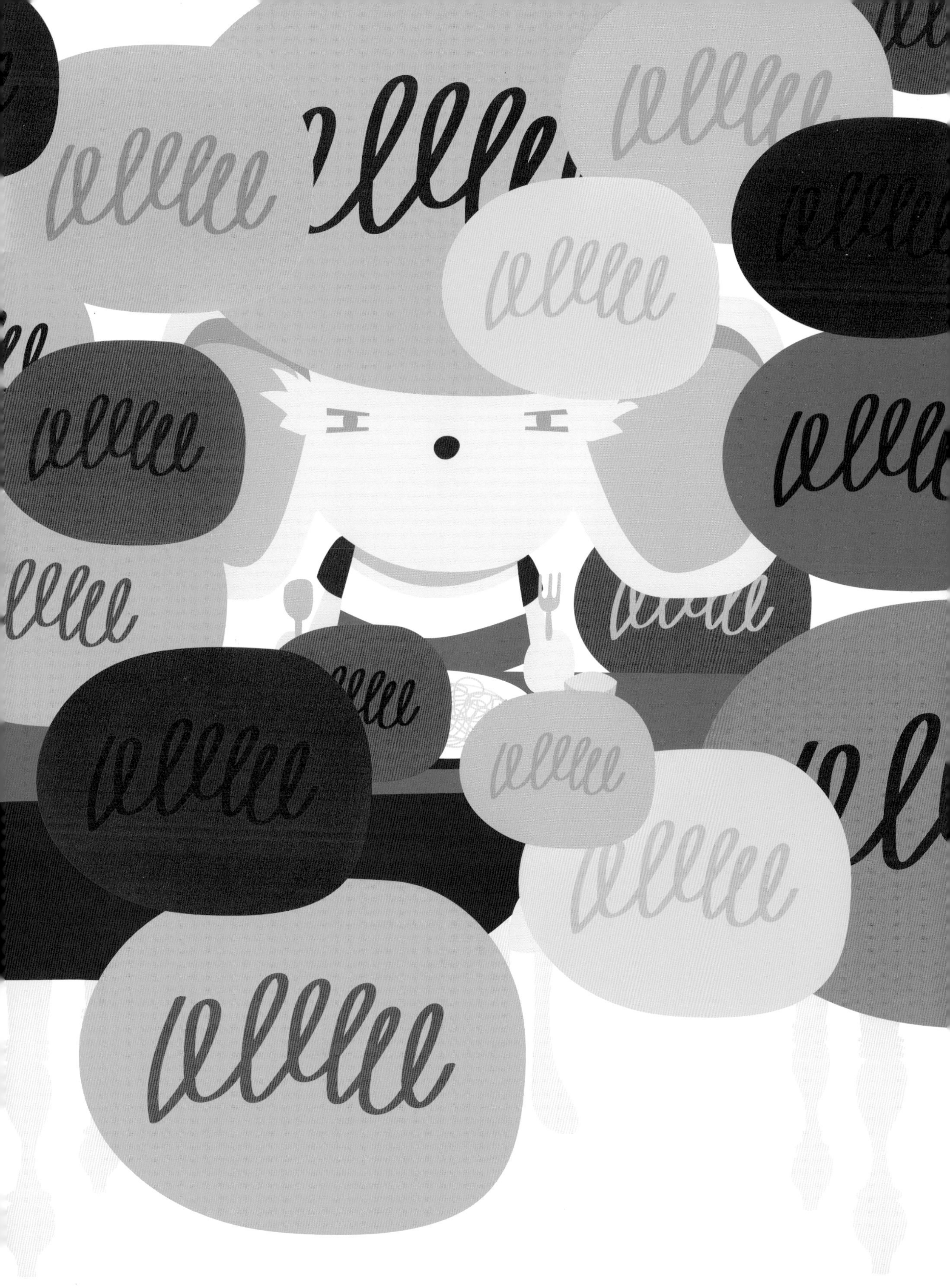

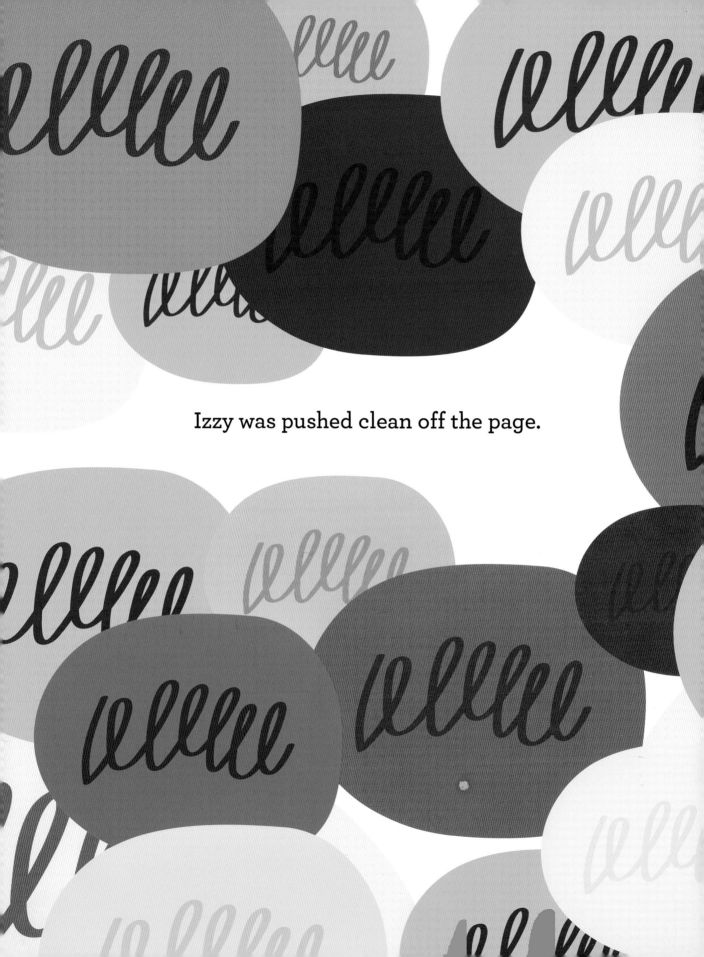

Izzy was pushed clean off the page.

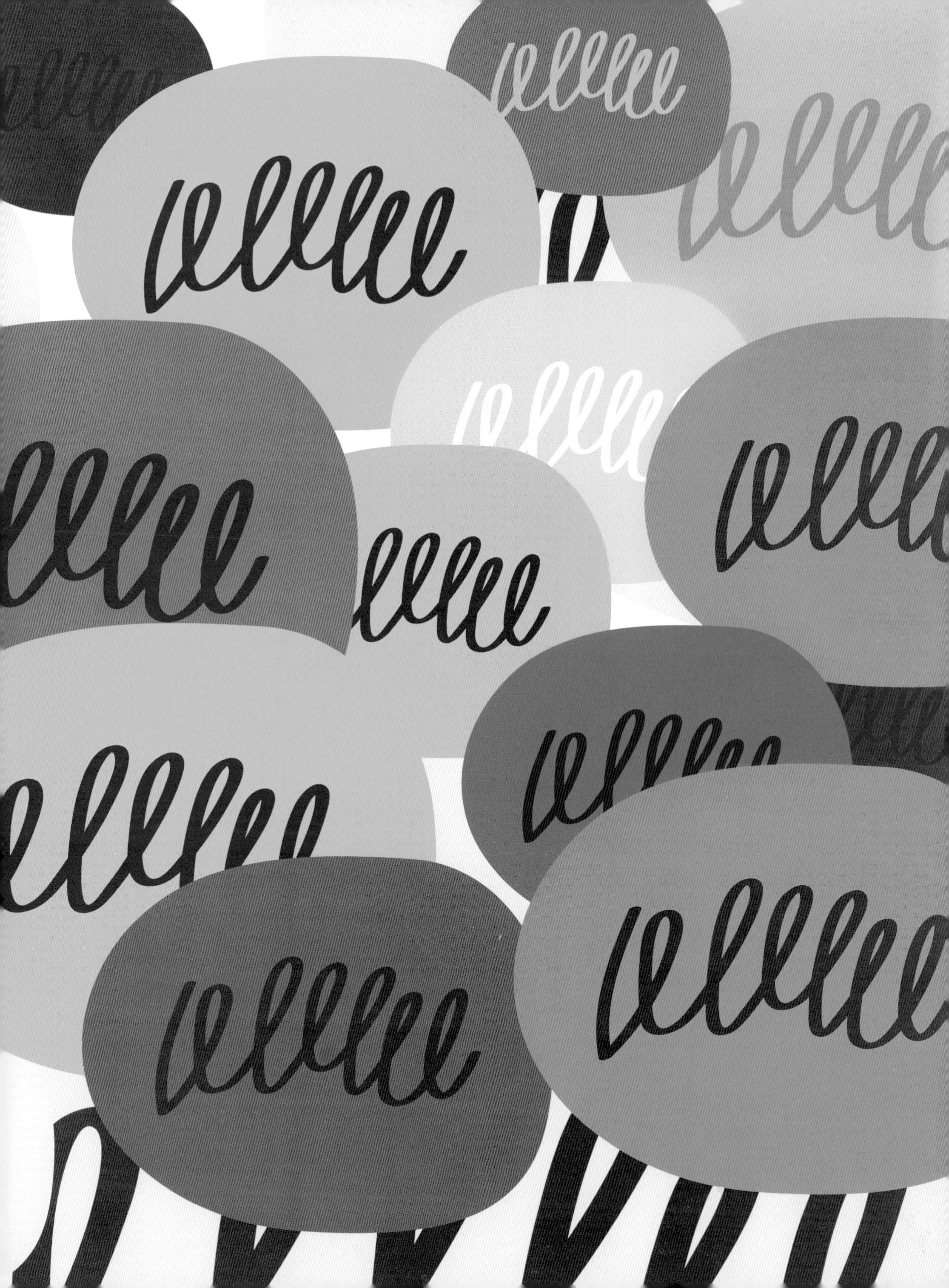

Something had to be done.

So she made her way to her secret spot.

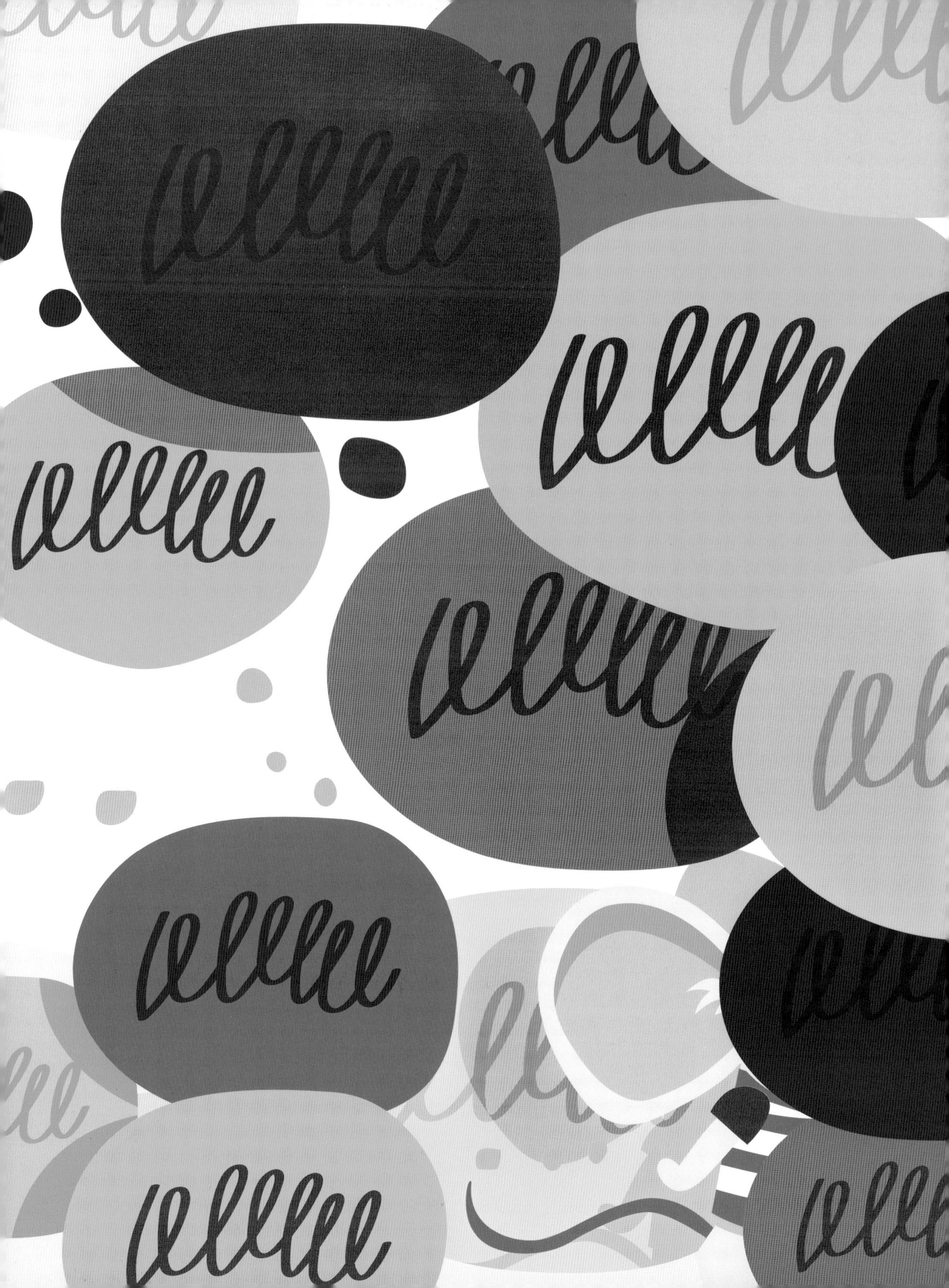

There was a little more space for all the bubbles.

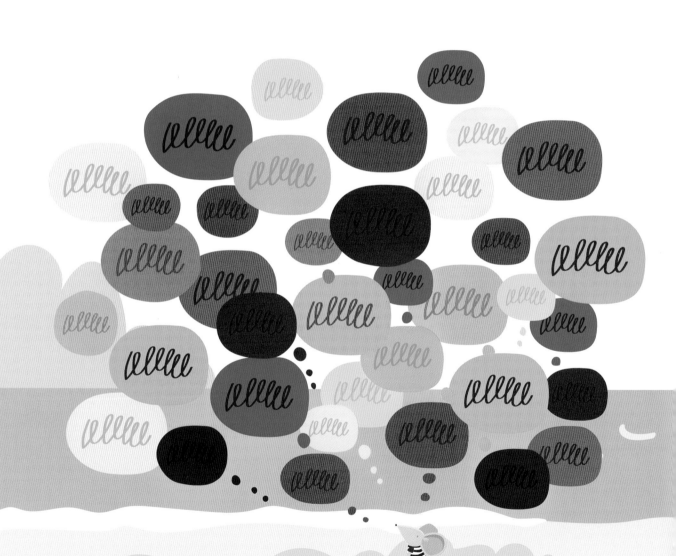

Izzy took a deep breath in.

Izzy let the deep breath out.

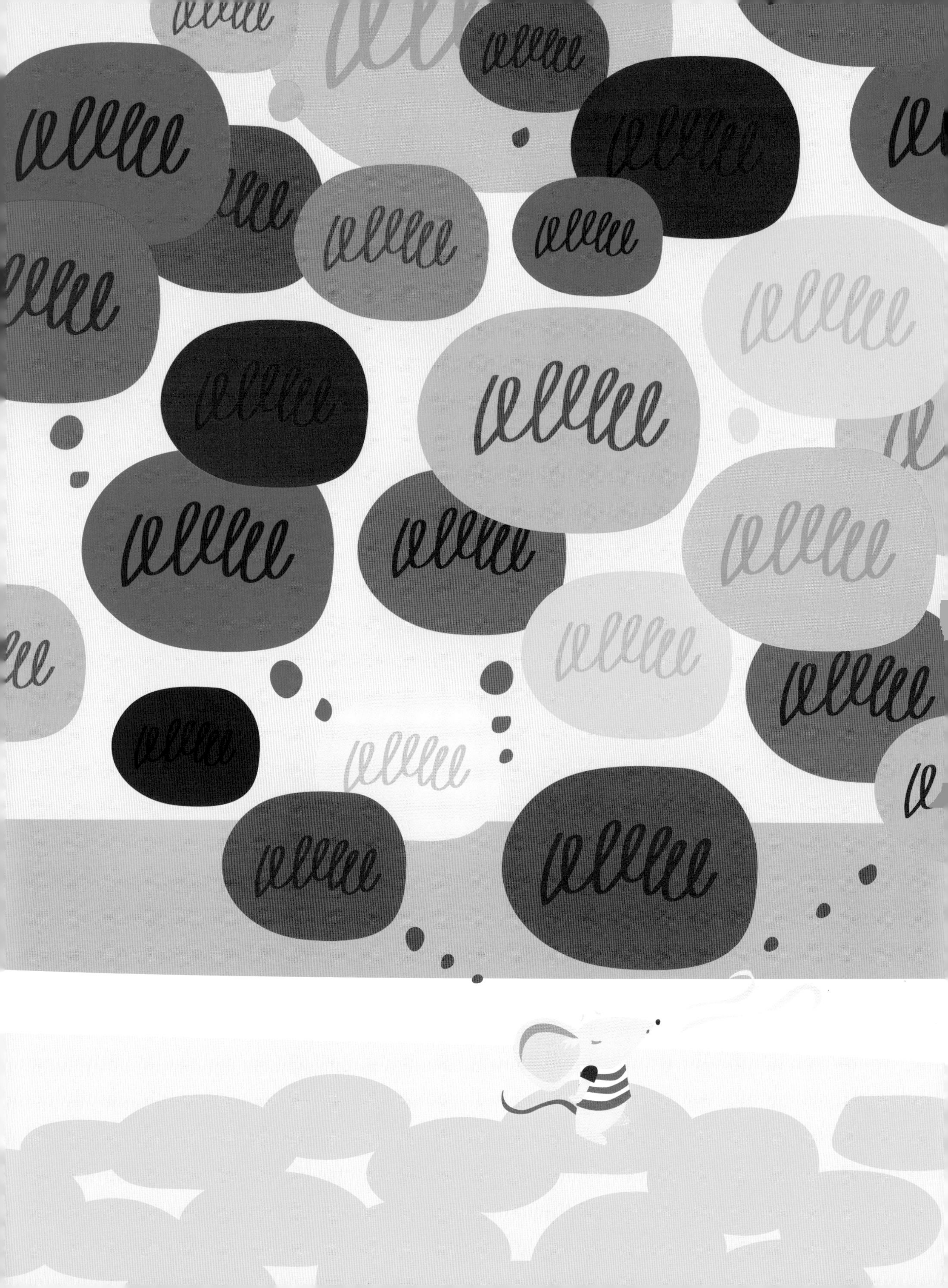

You can help Izzy.
Just blow gently on the bubbles.

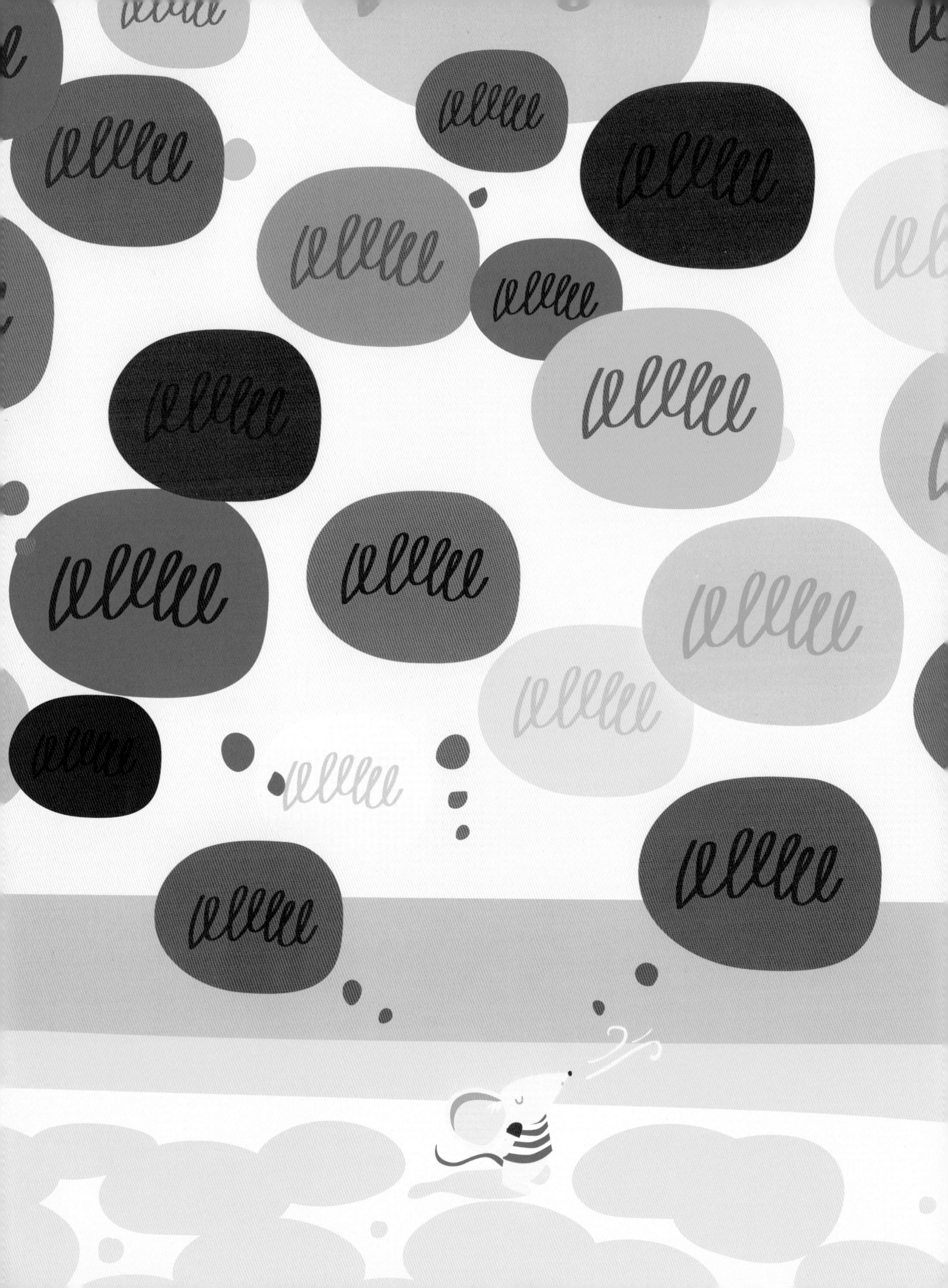

It's working!

Izzy's big, deep breath made
everything a little bit brighter.

— a —
LiTTLe MORE
MINDFUL

In the story you just read, Izzy the Mouse was able to find a state of peace by letting go of the thoughts that were taking over her day. This is one example of mindfulness, but there are lots of ways to practice this centering technique with your kiddos (you might find that you benefit as well!).

Wait, wait, wait. What is mindfulness, if you please?

Mindfulness is the practice of being aware in the present moment—aware of our thoughts, emotions and state of being, without judgment.

But what does that mean in kid-speak, for kids?

Mindfulness is simply paying attention. Kids can tune into their bodies, their senses, their minds, to reach a state of calm presence, making them feel light as a feather, or a puffy cloud.

Here are a few mindfulness exercises to try out. You can talk your kiddo through them in a calm, soothing voice. Feel free to add your own personality to them, the important part is presence.

EVERY BODY CALM

To begin, get into a comfortable position and close your eyes.

Take a few deep breaths to slow your breathing down.

Starting at the tips of your toes, relax each part of your body. Toes, then feet. Relax your legs, then your belly. Let go of any scrunching in your shoulders & arms. Wiggle your fingers until they calm down and rest. Then your neck, and your cheeks, your jaw and even your tongue.

Pause here, and be still for several minutes.

EMOTIONS in MOTION

Practice identifying emotions.

Look through books, and notice and talk about how the characters are feeling.

The more practice little ones get, the easier it is for them to identify and talk through their own emotions.

Sense-ATIONAL Time

In this exercise, have your kiddo tune into their senses.

After a few deep breaths, ask your little one to notice what they hear. What are all the sounds going on around them?

Go slowly, noticing takes a little time, sometimes.

This works with other senses as well. If you are eating a meal, try it out with tasting, or on a walk, ask what they see.

Silly Street is on a mission to help kids build character through play. Books of Great Character are just one part of our playful character-building world of activities & resources. For more, visit:

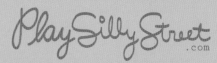

Published by Sourcebooks Jabberwocky, an imprint of Sourcebooks Kids
P.O. Box 4410, Naperville, Illinois 60567–4410
(630) 961-3900
sourcebookskids.com
Library of Congress Cataloging-in-Publication Data is on file with the publisher.
Source of Production: Leo Paper, Heshan City, Guangdong Province, China
Date of Production: March 2021
Run Number: 5021252
Printed and bound in China.
LEO 10 9 8 7 6 5 4 3 2 1